Originally published in the Netherlands 1989 by
Lemniscaat b.v. Rotterdam

First published in the United States 1989 by
E. P. Dutton, a division of Penguin Books USA Inc.

ISBN 0-525-44545-5
10 9 8 7 6 5 4 3 2 1

Printed and bound in Belgium
First American Edition

INTRODUCTION

All children have rights: the right to protection, to education, to food and medical care, and to much more.

Every child, no matter where he or she lives, has the right to grow up feeling safe and cared for: a simple thought, which few would openly challenge.

But, sadly, the reality is quite different.

Every day children are born who may never know the things more fortunate children take for granted. Many are exploited. Many cannot even grow up with their own families because their countries are ravaged by war. Some go hungry because there is famine; others will never have the chance to learn and grow; some cannot even play.

This is the year we celebrate the thirtieth anniversary of the declaration of the Rights of the Child – and remember how far we must still go to make that hope a reality. This is the year when the many nations of the world may finally ratify the Convention of the Rights of the Child – an enormous step forward to a better future for all the world's children.

This book is about the Rights of the Child: for children to look at, to share with a brother or sister, parent, teacher or friend; to laugh and to learn the joy that should belong to every child.

Audrey Hepburn
UNICEF Goodwill Ambassador

A CHILDREN'S CHORUS

Celebrating the 30th anniversary of the Declaration of the Rights of the Child

E. P. Dutton   •   New York

Principle One: We are the children of the world. No matter who our parents are, where we live, or what we believe, treat us as equals. We deserve the best the world has to give.

Principle Two: Protect us, so that we may grow in freedom and with dignity.

Principle Three: Let us each be given a name, and have a land to call our own.

Principle Four: Keep us warm and sheltered. Give us food to eat and a place to play. If we are sick, nurse and comfort us.

Principle Five: If we are handicapped in body or mind,
treasure us even more and meet our special needs.

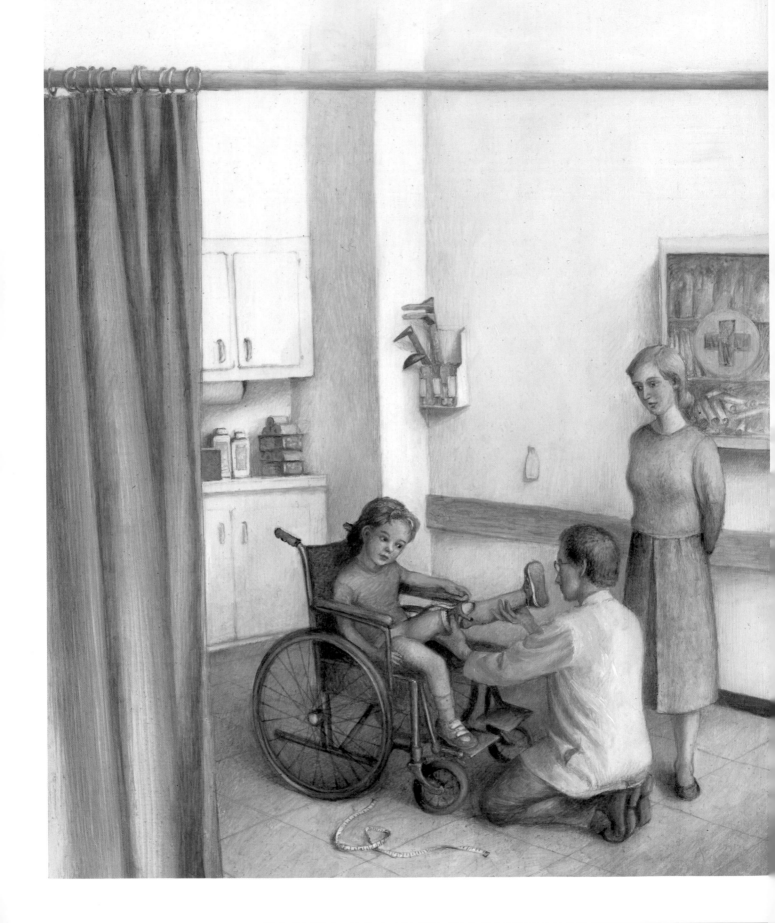

Principle Six: Let us grow up in a family. If we cannot be cared for by our own family, take us in and love us just the same.

ŠTĚPÁN ZAVŘEL * 1989

Principle Seven: Teach us well, so that we may lead happy and useful lives. But let us play, so that we may also teach ourselves.

Principle Eight: In times of trouble, help us among the first.
The future of the world depends on us.

Principle Nine: Protect us from cruelty and from those who would use us badly.

Principle Ten: Raise us with tolerance, freedom, and love. As we grow up, we, too, will promote peace and understanding throughout the world.

DECLARATION OF THE RIGHTS OF THE CHILD

as unanimously adopted by the General Assembly of the United Nations on November 20, 1959

PREAMBLE

Whereas the peoples of the United Nations have, in the Charter, reaffirmed their faith in fundamental human rights, and in the dignity and worth of the human person, and have determined to promote social progress and better standards of life in larger freedom,

Whereas the United Nations has, in the Universal Declaration of Human Rights, proclaimed that everyone is entitled to all the rights and freedoms set forth therein, without distinction of any kind, such as race, color, sex, language, religion, political or other opinion, national or social origin, property, birth or other status,

Whereas the child, by reason of his physical and mental immaturity, needs special safeguards and care, including appropriate legal protection, before as well as after birth,

Whereas the need for such special safeguards has been stated in the Geneva Declaration of the Rights of the Child of 1924, and recognized in the Universal Declaration of Human Rights and in the statutes of specialized agencies and international organizations concerned with the welfare of children,

Whereas mankind owes to the child the best it has to give,

Now therefore,

The General Assembly

Proclaims this Declaration of the Rights of the Child to the end that he may have a happy childhood and enjoy for his own good and for the good of society the rights and freedoms herein set forth, and calls upon parents, upon men and women as individuals and upon voluntary organizations, local authorities and national Governments to recognize these rights and strive for their observance by legislative and other measures progressively taken in accordance with the following principles:

PRINCIPLE 1   The child shall enjoy all the rights set forth in this Declaration. All children, without any exception whatsoever, shall be entitled to these rights, without distinction or discrimination on account of race, color, sex, language, religion, political or other opinion, national or social origin, property, birth or other status, whether of himself or of his family.

PRINCIPLE 2   The child shall enjoy special protection, and shall be given opportunities and facilities, by law and by other means, to enable him to develop physically, mentally, morally, spiritually and socially in a healthy and normal manner and in conditions of freedom and dignity. In the enactment of laws for this purpose the best interests of the child shall be the paramount consideration.

PRINCIPLE 3   The child shall be entitled from his birth to a name and nationality.

PRINCIPLE 4   The child shall enjoy the benefits of social security. He shall be entitled to grow and develop in health; to this end special care and protection shall be provided both to him and to his mother, including adequate prenatal and postnatal care. The child shall have the right to adequate nutrition, housing, recreation and medical services.

PRINCIPLE 5   The child who is physically, mentally or socially handicapped shall be given the special treatment, education and care required by his particular condition.

PRINCIPLE 6   The child, for the full and harmonious development of his personality, needs love and understanding. He shall, wherever possible, grow up in the care and under the responsibility of his parents, and in any case in an atmosphere of affection and of moral and material security; a child of tender years shall not, save in exceptional circumstances, be separated from his mother. Society and the public authorities shall have the duty to extend particular care to children without a family and those without adequate means of support. Payment of state and other assistance toward the maintenance of children of large families is desirable.

PRINCIPLE 7   The child is entitled to receive education, which shall be free and compulsory, at least in the elementary stages. He shall be given an education which will promote his general culture, and enable him on a basis of equal opportunity to develop his abilities, his individual judgment, and his sense of moral and social responsibility, and to become a useful member of society.

The best interests of the child shall be the guiding principle of those responsible for his education and guidance; that responsibility lies in the first place with his parents.

The child shall have full opportunity for play and recreation, which should be directed to the same purpose as education; society and the public authorities shall endeavor to promote the enjoyment of this right.

PRINCIPLE 8   The child shall in all circumstances be among the first to receive protection and relief.

PRINCIPLE 9   The child shall be protected against all forms of neglect, cruelty and exploitation. He shall not be the subject of traffic, in any form.

The child shall not be admitted to employment before an appropriate minimum age; he shall in no case be caused or permitted to engage in any occupation or employment which would prejudice his health or education, or interfere with his physical, mental or moral development.

PRINCIPLE 10   The child shall be protected from practices which may foster racial, religious and any other form of discrimination. He shall be brought up in a spirit of understanding, tolerance, friendship among peoples, peace and universal brotherhood and in full consciousness that his energy and talents should be devoted to the service of his fellow men.